© 2000 Children's Leisure Products Limited

Published by Geddes & Grosset, an imprint of
Children's Leisure Products Limited,
David Dale House, New Lanark ML11 9DJ, Scotland

ISBN 1 85534  681 8

Illustrations by Sue King,
Simon Girling & Associates, Hadleigh, Suffolk

Printed and bound in Indonesia

# first steps

# Jump!

by
Judy Hamilton

**GEDDES & GROSSET**

# The lion can roar. AARRGH!

# The seal can honk. HONK!

The gorilla bangs his chest.
  THUMP, THUMP, THUMP!

The parrot can squawk.
  SQUAWK!

The monkey can screech.
SCREECH!

But look at the kangaroo JUMP!

He jumps high in the air

and

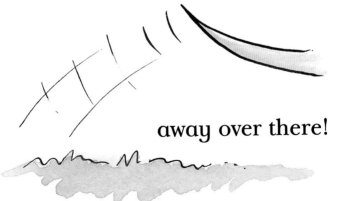

away over there!

Down by the pond, a little green frog.
Keeping very still, sitting on a log.

Spots a passing fly – yum, yum!
A tasty snack!

He JUMPS up, catches it

and then

JUMPS back!

Patricia has smart red shoes,
shiny, bright and new.

She comes across a puddle.
What should she do?

Her shoes must not get dirty,
    but the puddle is deep and wide.

She takes a deep breath,
    bends her knees ...

... and JUMPS to the other side!

Billy's having swimming lessons
  at the swimming pool.
"In you go!" says Teacher,
  "the water's nice and cool!"

"The water's DEEP!" says Billy,
"But I must learn to swim."

So he bends his knees, holds his
nose ...

... and JUMPS right in!

In the gymnasium, on the
 trampoline,
Stand Patricia and her friend
 Shareen.

First they wibble-wobble – it's
 not much fun.

But then they discover ...

how to JUMP

up

and down!

Laughing and squealing,
   they almost touch the ceiling!

"Wake up, wake up," says Billy's
    mum. But Billy curls up tight.
"I don't want to get up,
    It's the middle of the night!"

"Breakfast's ready!" says Billy's
  mum,
"Wake up, you sleepy head!"

Billy opens his eyes and smells
  the toast ...

... and JUMPS out of bed!

Douglas the dog is scratching,
there's something in his fur.
His master says, "Just look at
those fleas!"

"How did they get in there?"

Douglas knows the answer –
  they came from his brother!

They just JUMPED over, one
  after the other!

JUMP up!

JUMP down!

# JUMP way over there!

# JUMP like a frog, or a kangaroo!

# JUMP in puddles, if you dare!

# Bend your knees, stretch up tall,
# try to touch the sky!

JUMP! JUMP! and JUMP! again.

It's easy when you try!